To Claudia Bedrick
and Liniers.

-Decur

When You Look Up

Written and Illustrated by
DECUR

Translated from Spanish by
Chloe Garcia Roberts

Enchanted Lion Books
NEW YORK

Moving day had arrived.

Lorenzo's mother put her favorite plants in the car
so they wouldn't get hurt in the moving truck. Lorenzo took
his phone charger, favorite toys, and colored pencils.

Lorenzo was surprised to find
something in his new room.
What a strange piece of furniture!

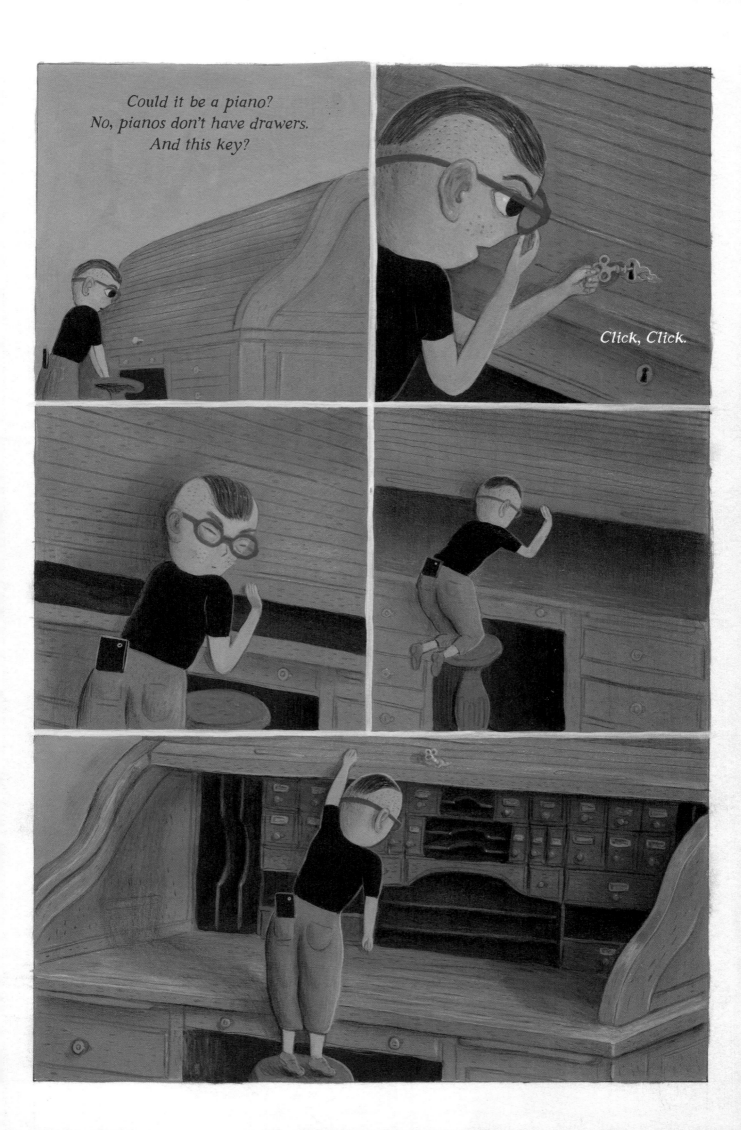

Every drawer Lorenzo opened smelled
like something he had never smelled before.

Somewhere between old wood and
something he didn't know how to describe.

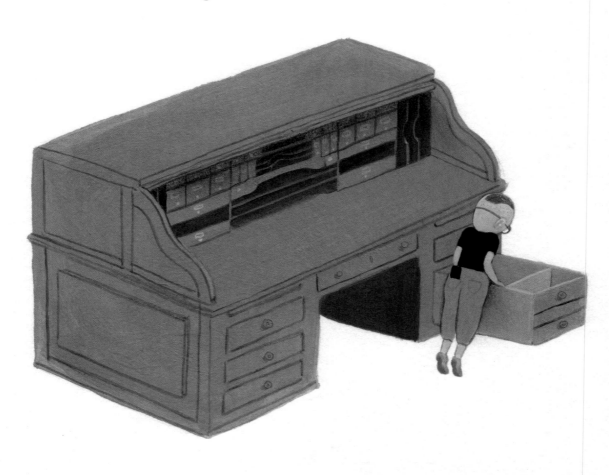

He felt frustrated that every drawer seemed to be empty.

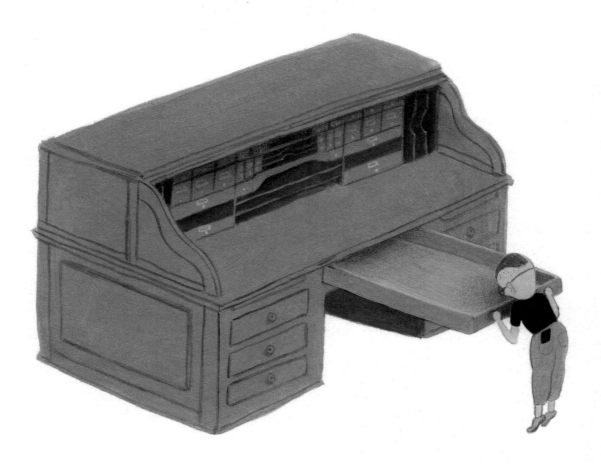

But he kept looking, intrigued.

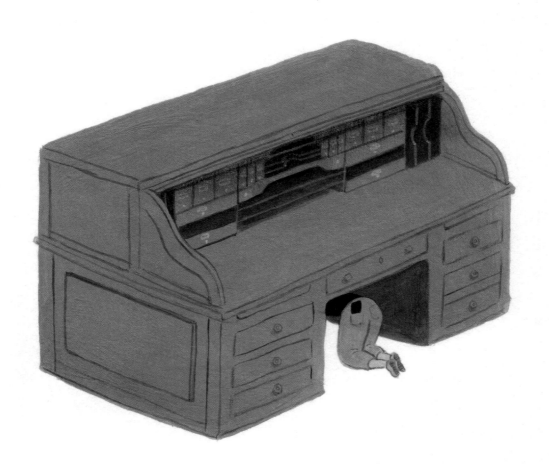

A secret door!
His heart beat faster at the thought
of all the toys that he might find.
But all he found was...

A notebook?

Lorenzo opened the windows and a delightful
breeze blew through his new room.

He opened the notebook.

THE
BRONZE
DRAGON

MY FRIEND PABLO AND I WERE TOSSING
A BALL BACK AND FORTH IN A VERY NARROW
PASSAGE FULL OF VALUABLE OBJECTS.
THE IDEA OF BREAKING SOMETHING TERRIFIED
AND FASCINATED US AT THE SAME TIME.

THERE WAS NOWHERE ELSE TO PLAY.
THE SPACE HAD NO WINDOWS AND THE CEILING
WAS SO HIGH WE COULD BARELY SEE IT.

THE GAME CONSISTED OF US THROWING A BALL
TO EACH OTHER WITHOUT ALLOWING IT TO DROP.
WE HAD GONE DAYS WITHOUT IT HITTING THE GROUND
EVEN ONCE, BUT PABLO WAS STARTING TO GET BORED.
SUDDENLY, HE THREW THE BALL BACK TO ME WAY TOO FAST.

I RETURNED THE BALL BACK TO HIM, TRYING NOT
TO HIT THE LAMP, BUT IT WAS SO TEMPTING...

I KNEW I WAS GOING TO BE IN A LOT OF TROUBLE.

WE STOOD THERE LOOKING AT THE DAMAGE WE HAD DONE TO THAT POOR LAMP.

THEN WE NOTICED THAT IT WAS MOVING.

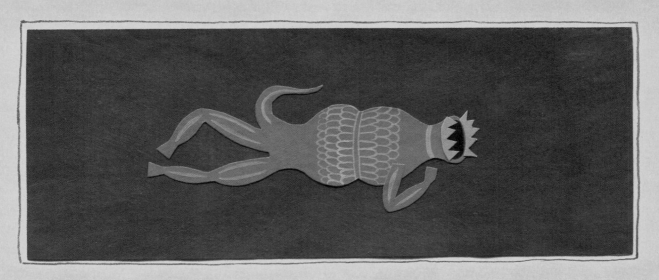

AND NOT ONLY THAT. SUDDENLY, THE LAMP TURNED
INTO OUR WORST NIGHTMARE...

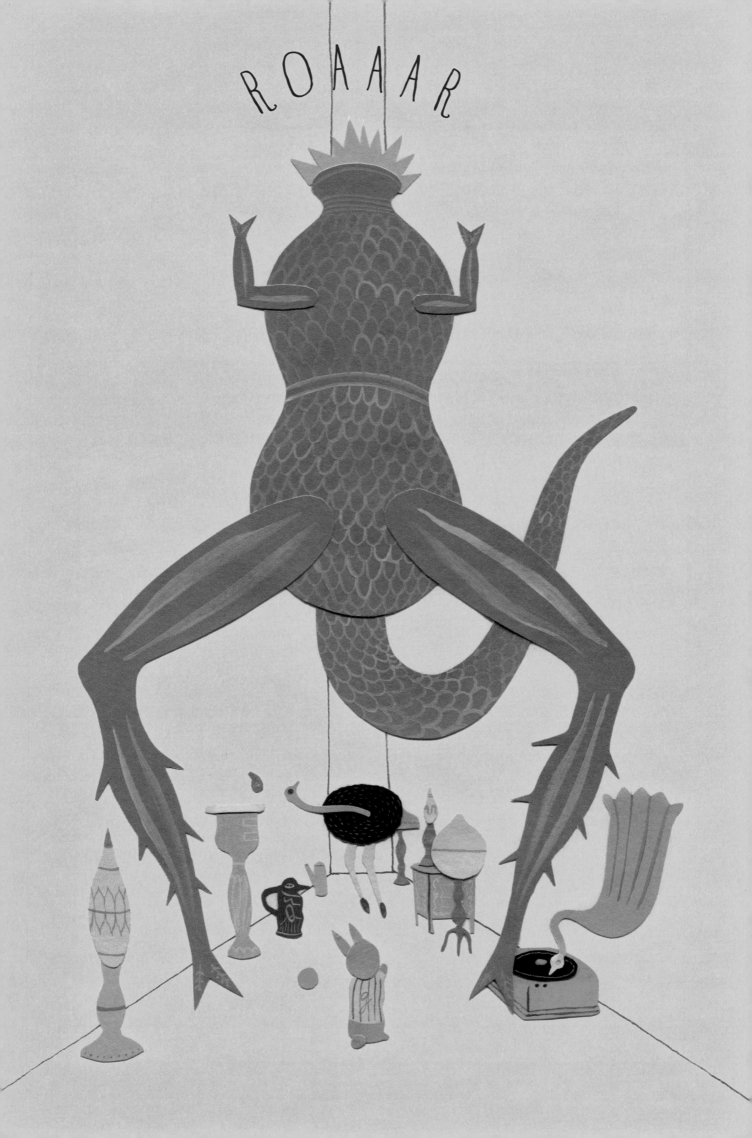

CAMOUFLAGING HIMSELF AMONG
THE OBJECTS, MY FAITHFUL FRIEND PABLO
DIDN'T HELP ME AT ALL.

IT APPEARED I WAS TRAPPED
WITH NO ESCAPE. BUT THEN,
AS IF BY MAGIC, THE WALLS BECAME
TRANSPARENT AND I FOUND MYSELF
IN THE MIDDLE OF A GREAT FOREST.

WITHOUT LOOKING BACK, AND WITH ALL
OF MY STRENGTH, I TOOK AN ENORMOUS
LEAP AND BEGAN RUNNING BETWEEN
THE TREES AND BUSHES.

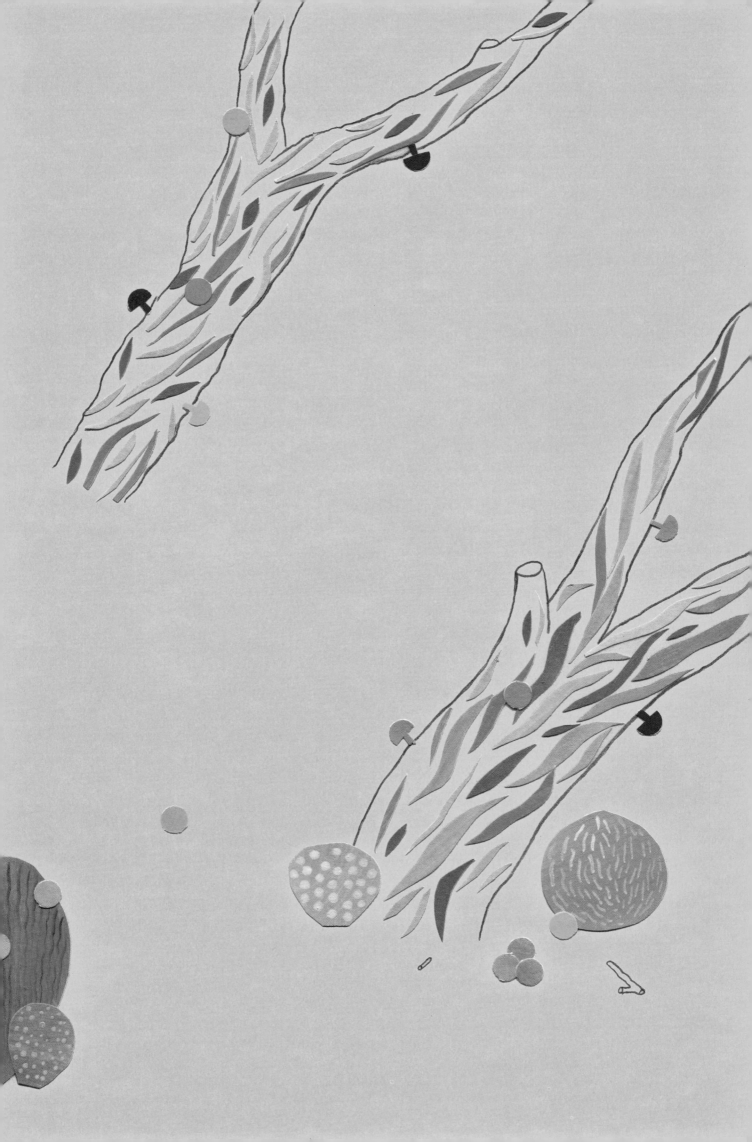

THEN, AS IF THINGS WEREN'T BAD ENOUGH,

THE GROUND
TURNED INTO GUM.

EVERYTHING SEEMED
TO BE AGAINST ME.

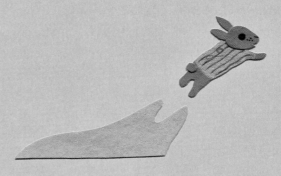

BUT TO GIVE UP MEANT
BEING EATEN ALIVE.

A LINE APPEARED IN FRONT OF ME AND I FOLLOWED
IT LIKE A ROAD. THE GROUND BECAME FIRM
AND I COULD RUN A LITTLE FASTER.

WHEN THE LINE ENDED ABRUPTLY IN A CORNER,
I THOUGHT MY LIFE WOULD END THERE, TOO.

I CLOSED MY EYES AND HELD MY BREATH. I FELT LIKE
THE DARKNESS WAS TAKING HOLD OF ME. I HOPED IT
WOULD BE OVER QUICKLY, SO I WOULDN'T SUFFER.
THE MOMENT SEEMED TO LAST FOREVER....

BUT I STILL DIDN'T HEAR ANY FOOTSTEPS BEHIND ME.
AFTER A WHILE, I WORKED UP MY COURAGE AND TURNED
AROUND, BLINKING MY EYES QUICKLY, LIKE SOMEONE
STANDING UNDER A WAVE THAT'S ABOUT TO CRASH DOWN.

FROM THE WINDOW, I SAW THAT THE MONSTER
HAD CHANGED INTO SOMETHING BEAUTIFUL.
IT WAS ALL OVER!
FINALLY, I COULD BREATHE AGAIN.

Lorenzo sat completely still, staring at the bird without understanding any of what he had just read.

He tried to zoom in with his fingers on the tiny rabbit.

But its size didn't change. It was then that he noticed that the drawings were bits of paper glued onto the pages.

Lorenzo! The moving truck is here. Please come down and help!
ALL RIGHT...

Lorenzo was about to head downstairs when something caught his eye.

Lorenzo's glasses made everything look sharper.
He noticed that one of the dragons on the chandelier
had a broken lampshade... It looked vaguely familiar,
but he wasn't sure why.

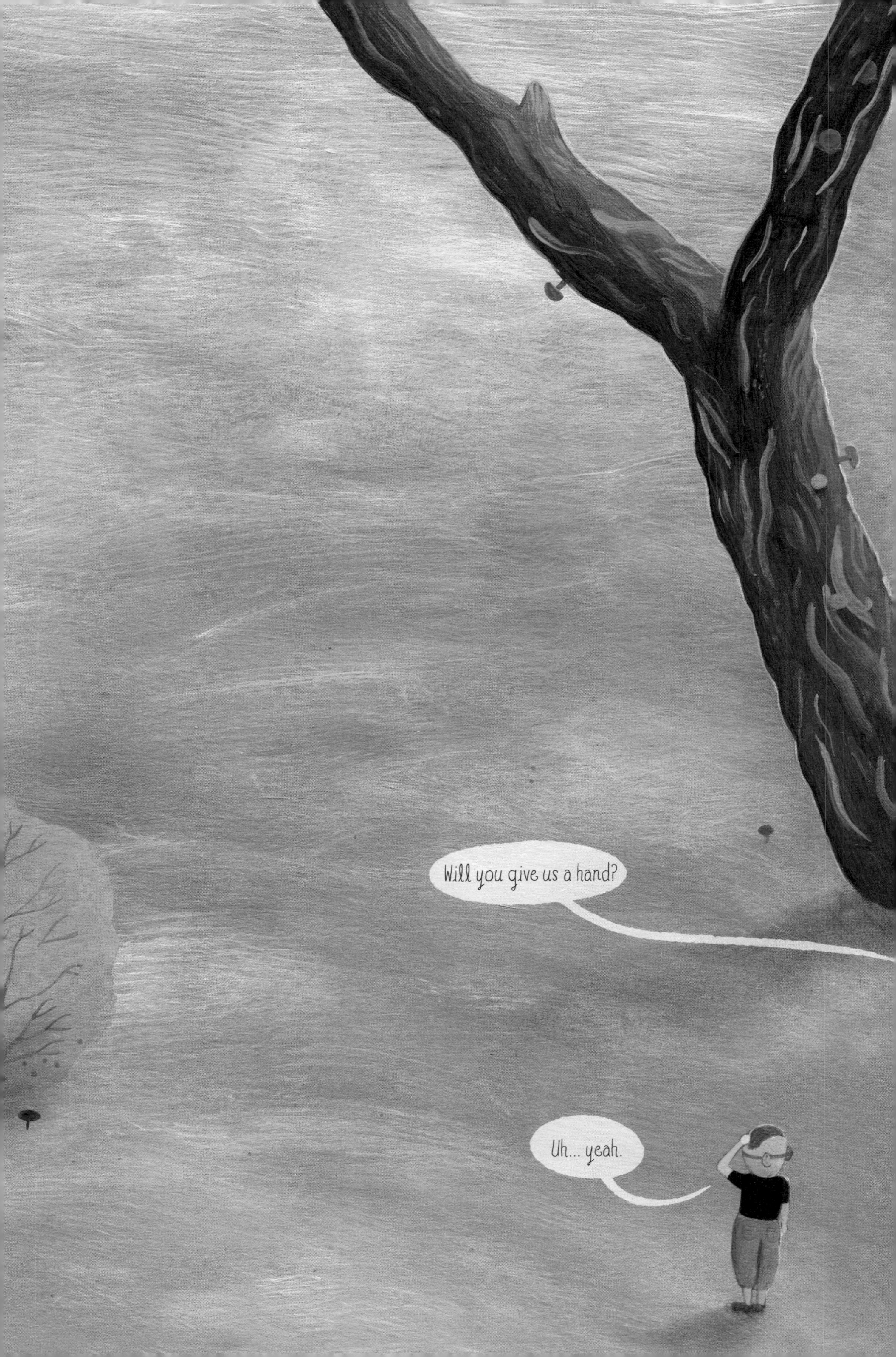
Will you give us a hand?
Uh... yeah.

In the morning, Lorenzo opened the notebook
to where he'd left off, removing the leaf that
he had placed there as a bookmark.

THE
BOOT
AND
THE
HAT

EVERYDAY, I CHECK THE AIR IN MY BICYCLE TIRES.
MY FINGERS CAN ALWAYS FEEL THE EXACT
PRESSURE NEEDED FOR A GOOD RIDE.

ONE DAY,
AS I WAS ROUNDING
A CORNER, A STRANGE
HAT APPEARED FROM
BEHIND A HOUSE.
WEARING THE HAT WAS
THE GIRL I LIKED.
IT WAS IMPOSSIBLE
NOT TO LOOK AT HER,
BUT I DIDN'T WANT HER
TO SEE ME STARING.
WHEN SHE LOOKED
STRAIGHT AT ME,
I TURNED AS RED
AS A BEET.

BUT SHE COMPLETELY IGNORED ME
AND MY HEART DEFLATED LIKE A TIRE.

JUST THEN, A SMALL, ANNOYING
DOG APPEARED OUT OF NOWHERE
AND BEGAN TO CHASE THE GIRL.
IT WOULDN'T STOP BARKING.

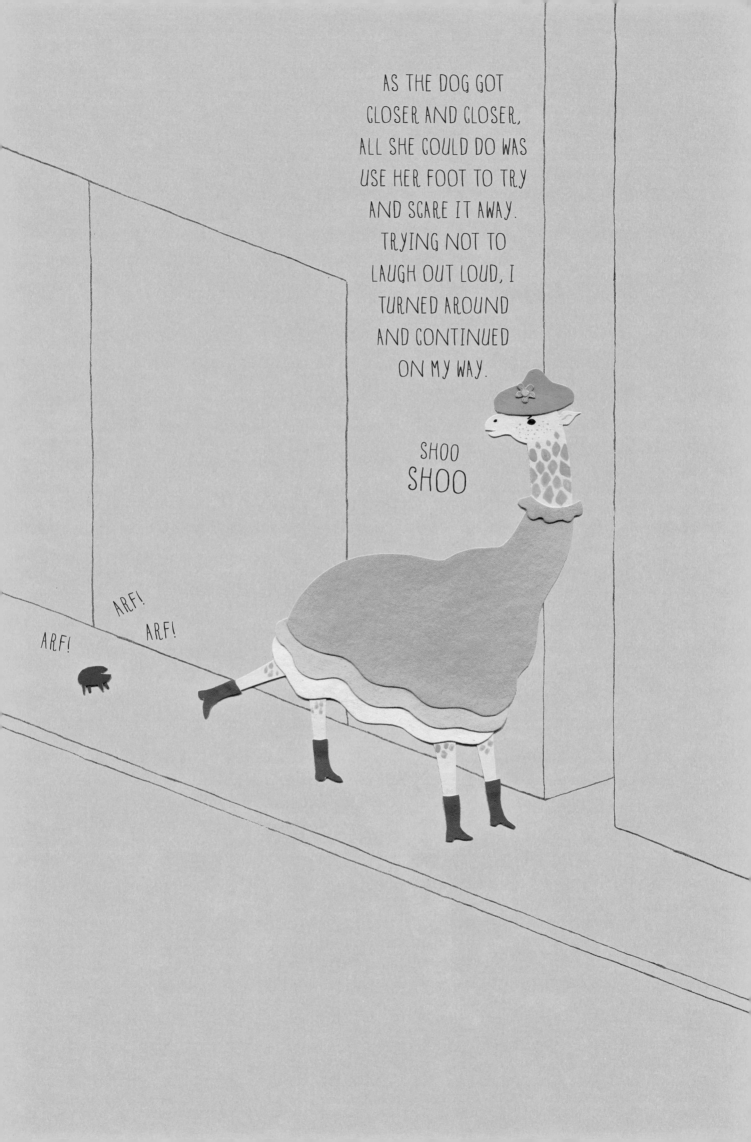

THEN THE WORST HAPPENED.

HER SCREAM WAS SO LOUD, IT SHATTERED
THE WINDOW OF A PASSING PLANE.

JUST MY LUCK.

MY HEART WAS BEATING FAST AS I MOVED IN
AND AIMED A TREMENDOUS KICK AT THE DOG.
IN THE BLINK OF AN EYE (THOUGH IT SEEMED
TO HAPPEN IN SLOW MOTION), THE DOG'S BUTT
SHOT UP AND AWAY AND MY BOOT FLEW OFF MY FOOT.

THE DOG GOT STUCK IN A CHIMNEY
AND MY BOOT ENDED UP WHO KNOWS WHERE...

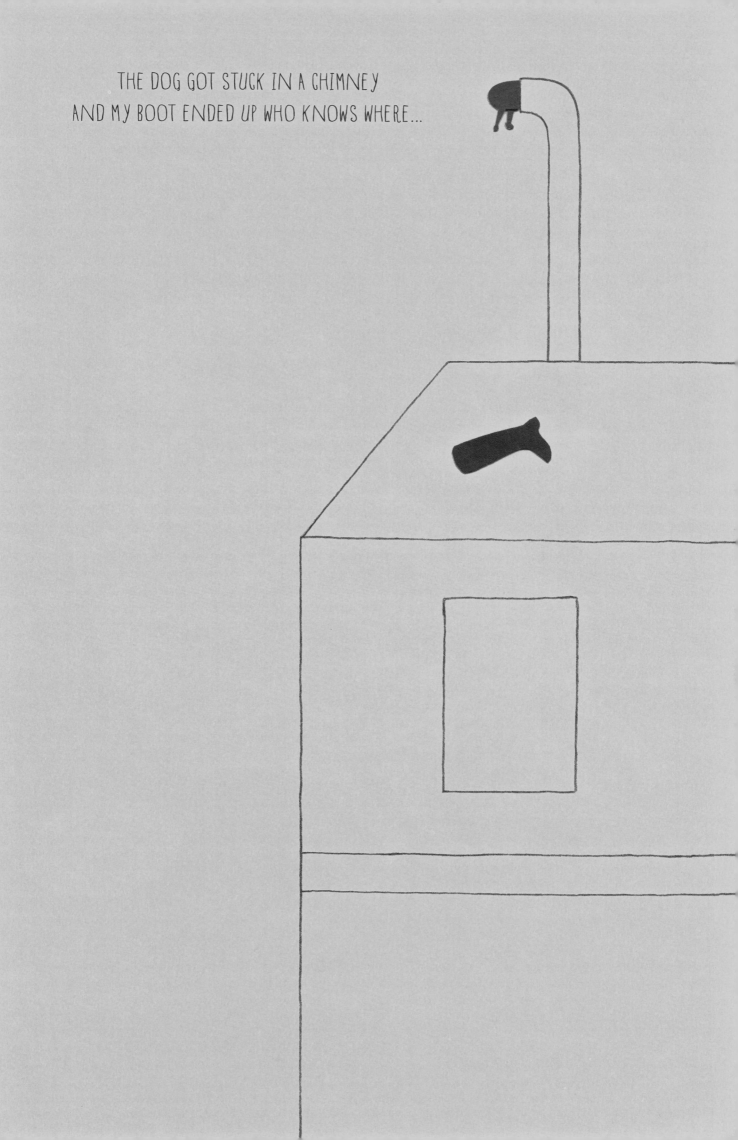

THE GIRL, WHO HAD FAINTED, WAS TURNING BLUE.
DID THE DOG HAVE RABIES? I WAS SCARED.
NOW IT WAS ME WHO WAS CALLING FOR HELP,
BUT THERE WAS NO ONE NEARBY.

I KNEW I HAD TO GET HER TO THE HOSPITAL, WITH NO TIME TO LOSE.
I DON'T KNOW WHERE I FOUND THE STRENGTH, BUT I HOISTED HER
UP ON MY SHOULDERS AND GOT BACK ON MY BICYCLE.

SHE WAS HORRIBLY HEAVY AND IT WAS HARD FOR ME TO PEDAL.

BUT THE FARTHER I WENT, THE STRONGER I FELT. SOON, SHE DIDN'T SEEM TO WEIGH AS MUCH, AND I COULD GO FASTER.

STRANGELY, SHE WAS GETTING LIGHTER AND LIGHTER.
I CHECKED TO SEE IF I WAS STILL CARRYING HER
ONLY TO DISCOVER THAT SHE WAS SHRINKING!

I NEEDED TO GET TO THE HOSPITAL AS SOON AS POSSIBLE
OR SHE WOULD DISAPPEAR!

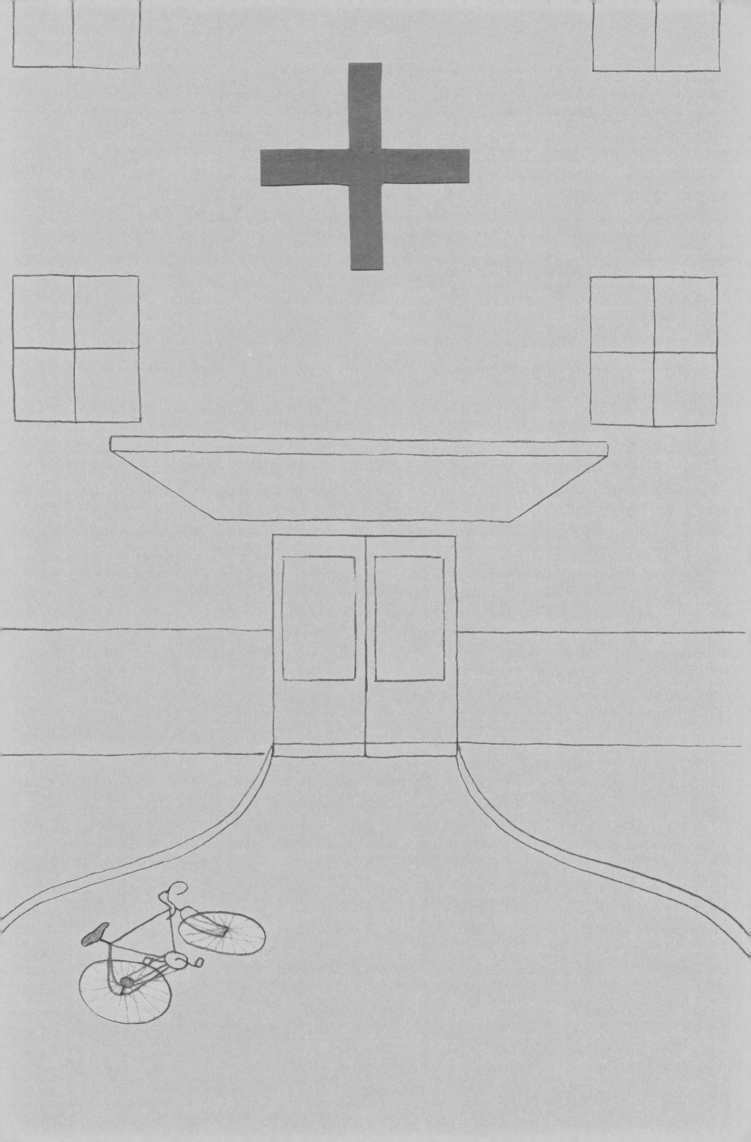

I HANDED THE GIRL OVER TO THE DOCTOR, CAREFULLY PUTTING
HER IN HIS HAND WHILE EXPLAINING WHAT HAD HAPPENED.

THEN SHE WAS THERE AGAIN, RADIANT AS THE SUN!
FOR THE FIRST TIME SHE LOOKED AT ME AND SMILED.

THE DOCTOR TOLD HER WHAT HAD HAPPENED AND SAID:
ONE DAY THIS WILL BE A SWEET STORY ABOUT HOW YOU TWO MET.

WE BOTH TURNED COMPLETELY RED.

THE NEXT MORNING AN ENVELOPE APPEARED UNDER MY DOOR.
I OPENED IT AND FOUND A BEAUTIFUL HANDSEWN BADGE.

Lorenzo mapped his way to town
and followed the directions.

Turn right, continue for 1,000 feet.

When Lorenzo entered the shop, he felt as if he had traveled back in time. The smells of cheese and salami mixed with the scent of old furniture. None of the old things in the store were unusual, but they were all new to Lorenzo.

To keep from being attacked, Lorenzo offered the dog a loaf of bread.

The dog's tail moved at the speed of light, calming Lorenzo.

He followed Lorenzo through town

and into the forest.

On his way home, Lorenzo decided to stop
and rest for a moment. He walked through the
grass with bare feet and then sat down to draw.

The mysterious dog with one eye stood guard
over him like a warrior. Lorenzo felt like the
most protected boy in the universe. The dog was
surely his first friend in this new place, but he
needed a name...

He'll have to stay outside, Lorenzo.

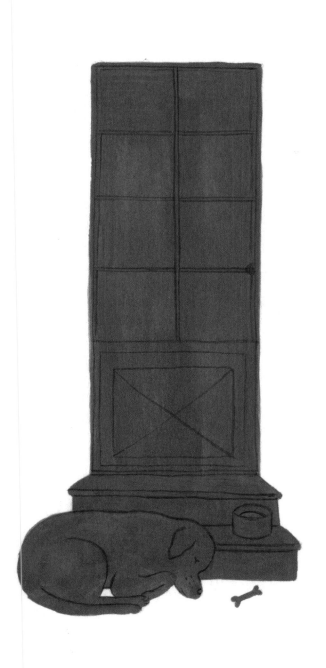

THE
FACTORY

WE WERE WORKING IN A FACTORY, ASSEMBLING STRANGE PARTS
THAT APPEARED ON A CONVEYOR BELT. WE DIDN'T KNOW
WHAT THE PARTS WERE OR WHAT THEY WERE USED FOR
AND WE HAD A BOSS WHO WATCHED OUR EVERY MOVE.

WE SPENT A LOT OF TIME TOGETHER, SO WE KNEW EACH OTHER WELL AND ALWAYS HELPED EACH OTHER. WITH THE RELENTLESS ROUTINE, WE DIDN'T HAVE MUCH TIME TO THINK, BUT WE DIDN'T REALLY WANT TO, EITHER.

OUR ONLY TOOLS WERE OUR BEAKS.
IF WE LOST THOSE, WE'D LOSE OUR JOBS AND OUR SONG.

TO MAKE THE MINDLESS WORK MORE BEARABLE,
WE TRIED TO ENTERTAIN OURSELVES BY JOKING AROUND.
BUT THE BOSS WAS ALWAYS THERE, SCOLDING US.

TWEET!

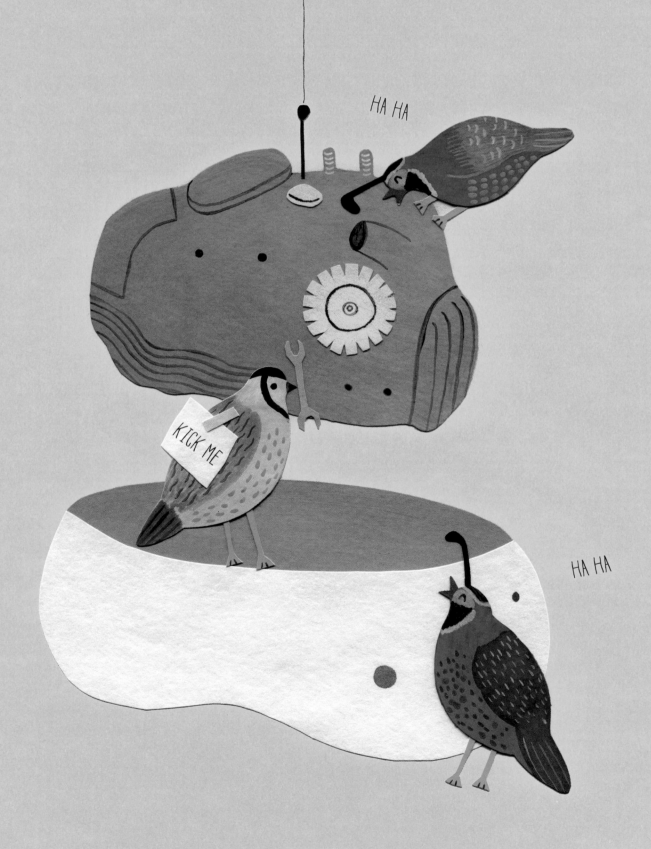

ONE DAY, THE CONVEYOR BELT STOPPED, THE PARTS DIDN'T ARRIVE,
AND WE HEARD A STRANGE SOUND THAT FRIGHTENED EVERYONE IN THE FACTORY.

GROAN

ALL THE PARTS THAT WE'D BEEN ASSEMBLING HAD COME TOGETHER
TO FORM SOMETHING THAT FILLED US WITH TERROR.

AFTER THE PAUSE, THE CONVEYOR BELT STARTED UP AGAIN AND
THE PARTS STARTED COMING OUT AGAIN. WE HAD TO GET BACK TO
WORK EVEN THOUGH THE THING WAS GETTING CLOSER.
SCARED, OUR BOSS RAN AWAY, BUT WE DIDN'T HAVE THAT CHOICE.
OUR NESTS DEPENDED ON US CONTINUING TO WORK.

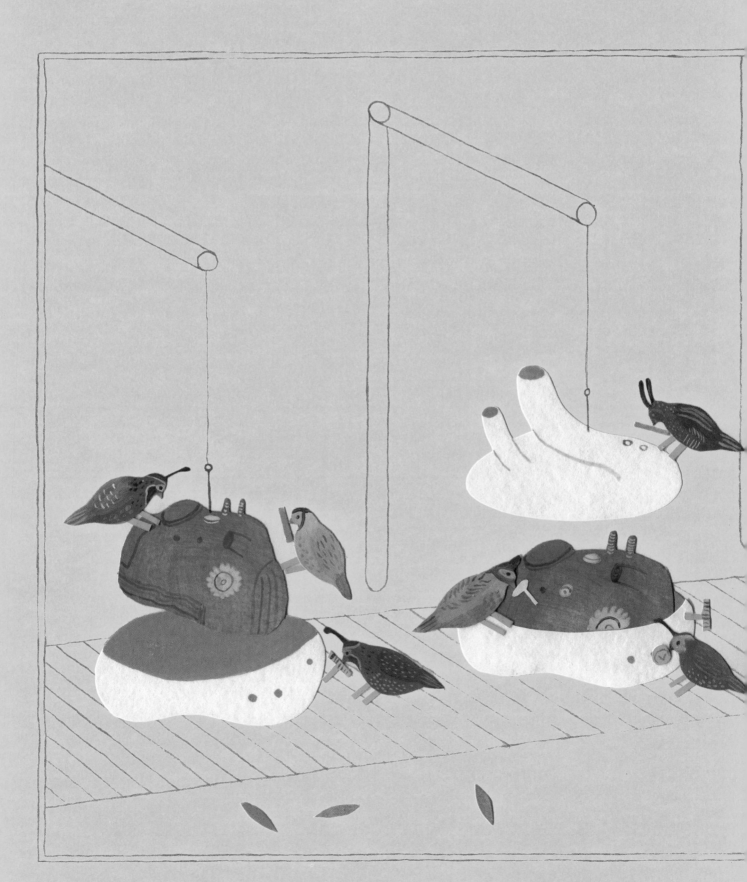

WE DIDN'T LOOK UP, BUT WE KNEW
SOMETHING AWFUL WAS HAPPENING BEHIND OUR BACKS.

EVERYTHING THE THING TOUCHED BURNED IMMEDIATELY,
LEAVING DARKNESS BEHIND IT.

FOR SOME REASON I'LL NEVER KNOW, THE THING PASSED ME BY
WITHOUT TOUCHING ME. BUT ALL MY FRIENDS DISAPPEARED.

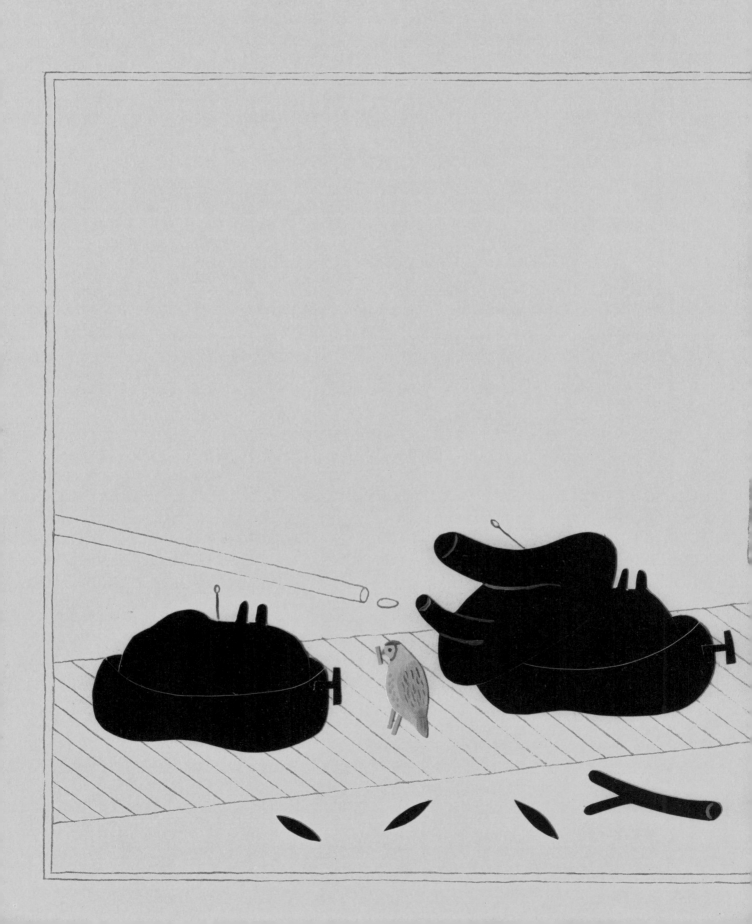

WHEN THE THING WALKED AWAY, I SAW THERE WERE MONSTERS
INSIDE OF IT, HAPPILY FEASTING ON MY FRIENDS.
IT WAS ONE NIGHTMARE INSIDE OF ANOTHER.

THE CONVEYOR BELT SPIT OUT NEW AND EVEN MORE SOPHISTICATED PARTS,
BUT MY TOOLS NO LONGER WORKED ON THEM.

THEN EVERYTHING WAS SUBMERGED IN DARKNESS.

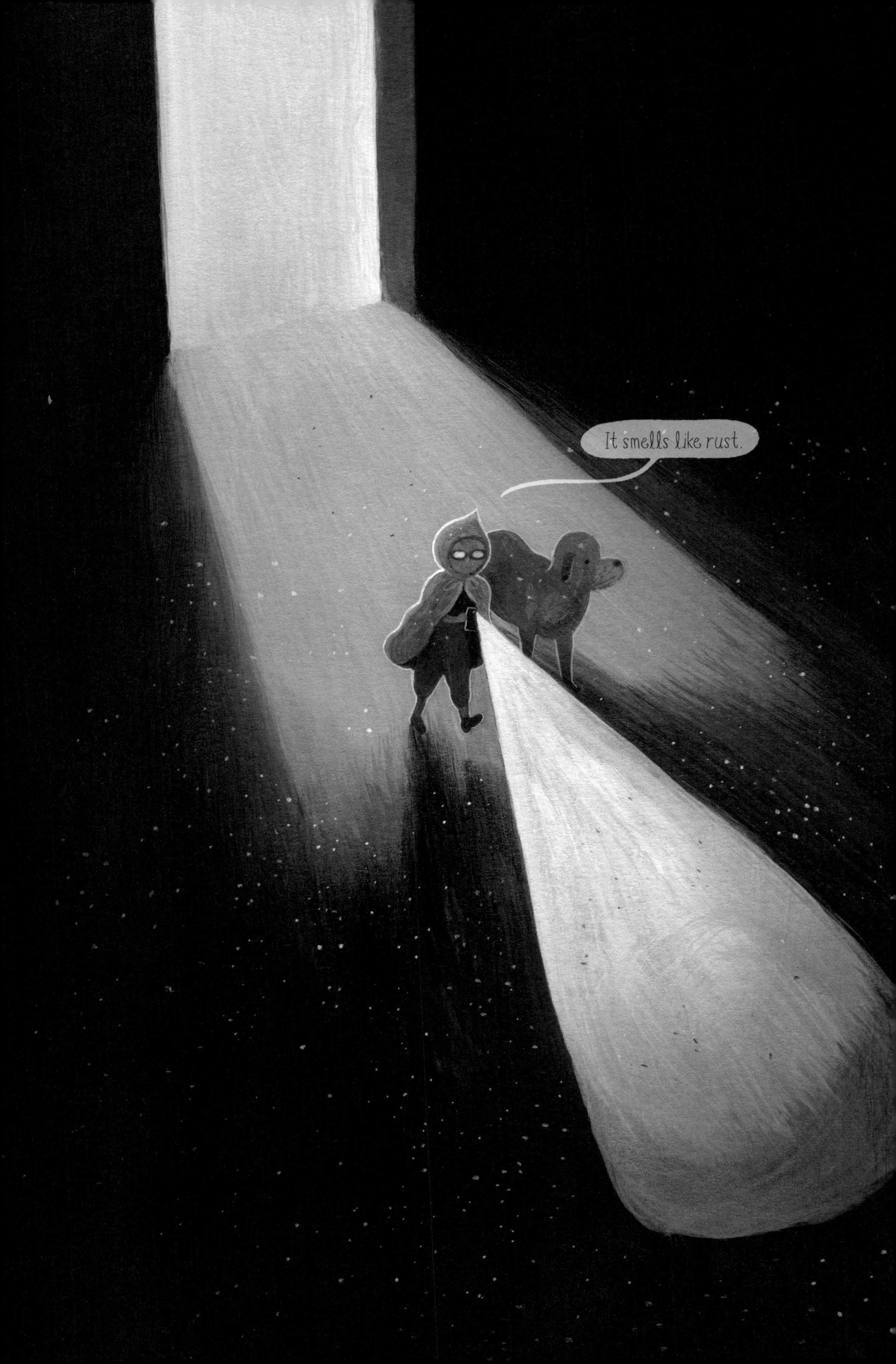
It smells like rust.

Lorenzo returned home soaked and muddy.
He washed up quickly and sat down to draw.

MY
DREAM
VOYAGER

I WAS FLOATING IN A TINY MATCHBOX
ON THE OPEN OCEAN.

ONE DAY, A HUGE SHARK SWAM TO THE SURFACE,
OPENED ITS MOUTH, AND SPIT OUT A TOILET SEAT, WHICH WAS
THE ONLY REASON I DIDN'T BECOME HIS NEXT SNACK!

I DECIDED TO WRITE A LETTER.

Hello,

I don't know where I am.
There is only the horizon as far as I can see.
Please find me.

-GREGORIO

I PUT THE LETTER INTO A BOTTLE AND
THREW IT INTO THE VAST EMPTINESS.

SPLASH!

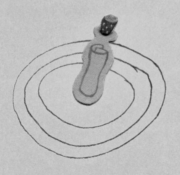

I FLOATED FOR WHAT SEEMED LIKE AN ETERNITY,
SO LONG MY WHISKERS TURNED WHITE.

ONE DAY, I HEARD A VOICE CALLING ME FROM FAR AWAY.

GREGORIO!

IS THIS YOUR LETTER?

IT IS!

THE MYSTERIOUS VOYAGER GENEROUSLY
SHARED HIS SUPPLIES WITH ME.

I DIDN'T WANT TO BE RESCUED,
I ONLY WANTED TO BE FOUND. SO WE SAID GOODBYE
AND HE SUBMERGED INTO THE DEPTHS ONCE AGAIN.
STILL, I FELT IN SOME WAY AS IF HE HAD
REEMERGED INSIDE OF ME.

I CLOSED MY EYES, A SMILE IN MY HEART.

When Lorenzo finished the chapter, he started to draw, but a nearby conversation distracted him.

When I was a teenager, I saved a girl who
had been bitten by a dog with rabies.

We fell in love that day
and later that night I dreamed
"The Boot and the Hat."

When I grew up, I worked with many of my best friends
in an automobile factory. One day a big explosion took away
those friends, my job, and my legs...